MARIA R. RIEGGER

Midnight Lasagna and Other Stories

**Eighth
House
Press**

Contents

Midnight Lasagna

I padded to the kitchen in my ratty slippers and gently opened the oven. Steam whispered out, carrying the feel-good smell of lasagna.

I inhaled deeply, and my mouth watered.

Screw it. I'm going to have some, I thought, as I took a small plate out of the kitchen cabinet.

I heard a soft sound, and immediately recognized it as the delicate shuffle of socked feet. I couldn't help smiling. Even though it was late, I loved it when he woke up at night; he usually came looking for cuddles.

I turned and melted at the sight of my seven-year-old, eyes puffy from sleep, holding his little stuffed piglet.

"I had a nightmare," he said anxiously. He still pronounced it "night-mirror."

"I'm sorry, my love. It's all right. It was just a dream."

He walked to the sofa and lay on it, face down.

"Why is life so scary?" he asked.

I sat down beside him and rubbed his back.

"Life is scary sometimes, but life is a lot of fun too," I comforted him as best I could.

He sat up and leaned against me. I put my arm around him and we gazed at the Christmas tree.

"Huh!" he gasped, pointing.

I looked at him, not understanding.

"There's a huge present under the tree!"

I smiled. "Yes."

"Is it for me?"

"You can take a look," I told him.

He ran over to the tree and knelt down. He grabbed the present and held it in front of his eyes, studying it as if it were something magical.

"It's for me!"

"Yes, yes it is."

He looked at me, mouth turned down.

"But Mommy, I didn't get you anything."

I smiled. "That's okay. I have everything I could ever want."

"Can I open it?"

"Not now. Christmas is only a few days away. I know it's hard to wait."

He slowly and gently put the present down, and continued gazing at it, as if he were afraid that he was dreaming and it would disappear any second.

"Hmmm, I wonder what it is."

I resisted the urge to let him open it early. "You'll only have to wait a few days."

He sat and looked out our living room window at the concrete jungle of apartment buildings, the sky overhead dotted with bright stars.

He turned his head and looked at me. "Is it late?"

"It's midnight."

"Mommy, what are you doing up?" he said in a tone that was almost as if he were scolding me.

"I'm having midnight lasagna," I answered with a smile.

2

He rubbed his face. "No fair," he said, yawning. "You get to stay up until midnight."

He wanted so badly to be a grownup, when all that brought was worry about bills and drudgery.

The sight of his cartoon-themed pajamas reminded me that he was still more child than adult.

"Believe me, my love, I didn't want to stay up this late."

"You couldn't sleep?"

"Well, I wanted to, but I had to stay up to finish the lasagna."

"You could've done it tomorrow."

"No, because I needed to cook it today, so we could eat it tomorrow. I don't want to have to eat out. We're trying to save money, remember?"

I immediately regretted my words, realizing the effect they could have on sensitive ears. My mind drifted for a few moments, remembering when I was my son's age. My family had theoretically had everything that we needed. A roof, clothes, food. But my mother had constantly made statements such as, "Oh, I don't know how I'm going to pay this bill. I had to dip into the savings account to pay the rent."

I would think, how much money is in her savings account? How long will it last us? I had little faith in my mother's ability to handle the family finances, and it had caused me a great deal of anxiety as a child, anxiety about money and resources that I had carried into my adult life.

Words are powerful weapons.

I determined not to cause the same anxiety in my son.

"We're doing fine," I said. "We have enough money for everything." I noticed the grave tone of my voice, and tried to lighten it. "The lasagna just took longer to put together than I had expected. And it smelled so good, I had to have some."

I returned to the kitchen to get my plate, and started dipping up a serving of lasagna.

My son continued to sit on the floor, mesmerized by the Christmas tree. My gaze drifted from him to the mismatched sofa and coffee table in our apartment, which were borrowed from friends.

I sighed.

Someday, we'll get new furniture, I thought for the hundredth time, when we've saved enough money. And we'll get a bigger house with a yard, and maybe even a swingset.

I continued dipping lasagna onto my plate, then hesitated.

"Would you like some?" I asked him.

Without answering, he got up and sat down at the dining table, which was really just a square table in the family room. To me, "dining table" meant something more formal, a long table with a leaf so that you could extend it for more people, with fancy chairs that had padded cushions for well-nourished rearends.

We had no room for that. We almost never had company, anyway.

He put his stuffed piglet on the table next to his placemat.

"Can I please have some water?"

"Yes, my love." I grabbed a glass and filled it.

I brought the glass and plates to the table and sat down.

In my usual fashion, I held my water glass out. In response, my son held his out and clinked his glass against mine.

"I love you," I told him.

"Love you too, Mommy."

"And merry early Christmas."

He grinned. "Merry early Christmas, Mommy."

The Mirror

Whenever she is preparing to go out, she always stays in front of the bathroom mirror for what seems like forever, as if she expects to turn into someone different the longer she stares at her own image.

At first she sighs, then purses her lips, as if she doesn't like what she sees.

She stands very still, plucking and lining, shading and painting.

She hardly ever notices me. I hide just outside the door, peeking one eye into the bathroom. She leans over the sink, so close to the mirror that she almost touches her twin.

Done with the plucking, she fluffs her hair, then smooths it, indecisive.

Next, she places her hair in front of her shoulders, reams of black silk cascading forward. Then she brushes it all away, so it falls down her back, almost to her waist.

She moisturizes and applies a cream that is almost the exact shade of her skin (*why bother?* I think).

Now she's not moving at all because she needs to line her eyes juuuust right. She traces dark lines around her eyes with a black pencil, making them pop out even more from her lean face.

She leans her torso back, raises her eyebrows, and cocks a

sideways smile, and I know that she is pleased with her work.

Then she spends an inordinate amount of time choosing the color of her eye shadow.

She almost chooses a bright blue, then shakes her head and goes for the tried-and-true deep charcoal (it's nighttime, after all!), which she applies expertly over her eyelids and just underneath her brows. Now, she has officially metamorphosed from my mother into an Egyptian goddess.

Now I know she'll only apply a light lip gloss to her mouth. If she had left her eyes unshadowed, she would go for a deep red or purple lipstick. I've heard her say that a bright color on her lips paired with a bold eye shadow makes her look like a clown.

She stays extraordinarily still, keeping her eyes unnaturally open while she applies mascara, sweeping the lashes up, careful not to brush them against her eyelids. Once she did that and said a curse word; then she had to remove all her eye shadow and start again.

But this time she's spot-on.

She looks at her image in the mirror and smiles. Her eyes crinkle a bit and the lines around them appear more pronounced. Even with the lines, when she smiles she easily looks ten years younger.

One time, the clerk at the grocery store asked her for her ID when she bought wine and she was happy for the rest of the day. It was because she was smiling, I told her.

"I'm thin, so people think I'm young," she once said to me. "Then they see my eyes and they know."

"Know what?"

"That I'm not young anymore."

My heart had seized at the thought. I didn't want to think about her aging. Aging meant creeping more closely toward the inevitable. Toward death.

But she had seemed blase about it. "Children are supposed to outlive their parents," she had said.

I didn't want to think about her leaving me. Where would I go?

"By the time I'm gone, you'll be grown up and on your own," she had said.

"But I don't want to separate from you," I had told her. "I want to live with you, even when I'm a grown-up."

She had immediately stopped what she was doing, and bent down to look me in the eye.

"You don't have to do anything you don't want to do," she had said. "You can always live with me." Her demeanor had automatically become lighter, and she had smiled mischievously. "So don't worry! Now let's get some of that cake that you like!"

Now, she smiles at herself in the mirror, apparently satisfied with her appearance. Lastly, she applies a clear pinkish lip gloss and then admires all of her work.

I know she's about to leave the bathroom. I scurry away so she won't see me spying. This time, however, I'm not quick enough.

"Hey, I see you there, goofball!" I hear her as I turn to run.

I turn back around and she approaches, wrapping me in a gentle embrace.

"What time will you be home?" I ask.

"Probably after you're asleep, but not *too* late. Office Christmas parties are usually boring." She boops my nose with her finger. She stands up, her knees popping, and walks toward the door.

"Be safe, Mom," I call.

"Always safe, sweetheart," she says, half-turning around and giving me her ageless smile. "Your sister will have dinner ready in a few."

She blows me a kiss and leaves.

I smile, because I've already decided that I will wait up for her, no matter how late she comes home.

A Night Out (In)

Full war paint,
   Dark red lipstick,
   Perfectly smoothed hair,
   Mile-high heels,
   Tummy sucked in,
   Skirt straight,
   Shoulders back,
   No slouching
   because the masses don't care if you're tired.
   Polished nails,
   Gold jewelry,
   So what do you do?
   Where are you from?
   Must be ready
   with prepackaged answers.
   I'm so witty,
   ha ha ha!
   All that's no match for
   Sweatpants,
   With pockets!
   Thick socks,
   A fresh face,

Hair pulled back in a mess,
Feet up on the furniture,
Back sinking into the cushions,
Coffee with a book,
SILENCE.
Dog at your feet,
Relaxed frown,
Not being forced to smile (my face hurts!),
Getting a snack whenever you want,
With no one watching, judging,
SILENCE.
No questions being darted your way,
No pressure to engage.
The quiet night an old friend,
And did I mention,
SILENCE.

To FOMO or not to FOMO?

Almost everyone around me appears to have FOMO, the dreaded fear of missing out. And it's even worse around the holidays.

Oh no! they think. I don't have any plans for the weekend, yet. Whatever will I do? I must fill every minute with something. I'll do brunch, then a music festival, followed by a pub crawl, then dinner, then a movie...

It's too much! Me? I don't get FOMO. In fact, if I do make plans, then I get FOMO of another kind. I get the fear of missing out on my own company.

That's right. When I'm alone in my home, you see, I have everything to myself. No noisy restaurants, no blaring music forcing me to scream to be heard. No jampacked bars where I'm constantly jostled and elbowed at best, cursed out at worst.

And don't even get me started on the money. $15 for a glass of wine? Why am I here again and not at home in my pajamas, partaking of a solitary, noise-free cup of tea?

Human connection is important, indeed (how else would I learn how to depict real dialogue in my writing?). But what about standing inside holding a cup of coffee, roasted exactly how YOU want, the steam wisping upward and warming your face, as you gaze through your window and watch a squirrel in your garden eat an acorn, rolling it back and forth in his tiny hands? Or watching a mama bird fly up a tree, bringing her youngling some food? I get you, mama, always thinking about your baby.

Or how about watching your dense dog chase a leaf? Or run back to the house all pleased with herself after barking (again) at the mailman?

And when you finish a good book and slowly close the cover, pondering the significance of everything you've just read. And you lean back on the sofa, feeling the softness of the cushions as your back sinks into them. You stretch out your arms and legs, not caring whether your shirt rises and exposes your tummy, because you are alone.

And your mind is clear and you can think, because you are alone, with no static, no interference, no one demanding your attention and begging you to make a decision.

That's a perfect night out. Or, rather, a night in.

Mime Attack: A True Story

Picture it: Barcelona, wintertime, around the year 2000. I was hardly more than a kid, working during the day and gallivanting around castles and cathedrals during the weekends.

My British friend was in town, and we ambled along Las Ramblas, Barcelona's pedestrian walkway that leads through the *Barrio Gotico* to the sea.

As we did so, chatting along the way, I took in the numerous holiday decorations that lined the shops, as well as the various street performers along Las Ramblas.

A certain mime, who stood very still on top of a box that served as a pedestal, was dressed in some type of old-fashioned costume, complete with a hat and long coat. His skin was painted silver; he seemed an alien not of this world. I was continually drawn to him, such that my eyes were glued to his face, almost daring him to look at me.

You see, at the time I called Barcelona home, and I knew that the mimes (who popped up everywhere!) never talked or moved. They couldn't (as far as I knew); that was part of the schtick. And so I glared at him defiantly. And while my gaze was locked on this particular mime's face, all the while listening to my friend next to me talk, the mime's eyes darted back and forth. Indeed, his eyes were the only part of him that moved. They shifted back and forth, from staring out at Las Ramblas then back to me, Las Ramblas, back to me, Ramblas, me —

"AAACK!" the mime screamed the second before I passed in front of him.

"AAAAAGGGHHH!" I screamed, cowering away in a near-fetal position, as he lunged toward me, arms outstretched, stopping just short of my shoulder.

My cries were heard throughout Las Ramblas. And, to this day, I have never since approached or even looked at a mime.

Keeping Up with the Joneses

I open the front door to my apartment and immediately begin opening my mail.

Oh no, I think when I see the red Hallmark envelope.

Another greeting card from my *mother.*

She insists on marking every occasion, from Halloween to St. Patrick's Day, even though we're not Irish. Of course, there was no way she would neglect to mark Christmas as well.

"Did you get my card?" she would ask me in about a week.

Isn't the point of sending these cards to let people know you're thinking about them? Or is the point rather to get acknowledgement for your act?

For her, it's less about the message and mostly about keeping up appearances.

"Why does everyone insist on keeping up with the Joneses?" I muse out loud.

"Everyone expects you to have a huge house, change your car every two years, have the right job, the right partner, take the right vacations —"

I sigh. 'Right' according to them, of course. What's better? To be miserable but have 'status' or to be happy and not have 'status?'

Nobody should have to think about the answer to that.

I open the Christmas card and glance at it. I hesitate, then place it on my kitchen table. My apartment didn't have a formal dining room. I always thought that those were a waste of space. How often would it get used, anyway?

My mother calls me occasionally, just to see how I am doing, but we rarely talk about anything substantive. That is how I prefer it.

I lean against my kitchen counter and shake my head.

Sorry I *only* live in an apartment, I thought, that I prefer to travel rather than be house poor, that I don't have a gaggle of children, that I stay in most nights and read to feed my brain instead of go out and engage in vapid activities with superficial people who live cookie-cutter existences.

I pretend to straighten an imaginary tie and have an imaginary conversation out loud.

"I'm John, and this is my wife Jill, and our son Jack. He just got into Harvard. Well, hello, I'm Tom, and this is my wife Tracy and our son Tim, and he just got into Georgetown. Cue the debate over whether Georgetown is an Ivy League school. *Who cares?*"

I turn around and reach into the cabinet for a glass, then fill it with water.

The other day my mother asked me why I didn't get a bigger house with a bigger yard. I asked her why I needed a bigger house and yard. She couldn't answer.

But the answer for her was clear. She wants me to have a bigger house because *she wants me to have a bigger house*, so that she can tell people, my daughter lives in a big house.

I purse my lips, frustrated. To her, a big house is a sign of status.

I'm an embarrassment to her. That's why she doesn't talk about me at parties.

Oh well, I don't care. Why should I? I don't go to parties. I smile, even though there was no one to see.

I don't have a fear of missing out. I don't have a fear of rejection. I have a fear of living a monotonous life, without experiencing anything, without creating anything.

I live life any way I want it.

Dirty Dishes

I won't remember dirty dishes and piles of laundry,
   Or dust bunnies lurking in dark corners,
   Or fingerprints on a window.
   Or a stray sock on the bathroom floor.
   I don't care too much about a cheap broken glass,
   That slipped through your small fingers
   During your first attempts at independence.
   What I will remember instead:
   An over-the-shoulder I love you
   As you ran to join your friends on the playground.
   A late-night snuggle because you woke up after a nightmare.
   An unsolicited kiss on my cheek.
   An unexpected phone call.
   You microwaving me a cup of coffee in the morning.
   Reading aloud to each other before bed.
   Short trips exploring new cities.
   Uno games during dinner.
   Late-night video game time,
   You killing a whole squad just to go get my reboot card.
   You introducing me to new things,
   Because who says adults can't learn anything from kids?
   Your off-the-cuff statements: "We're a lot alike, Mom."

Even your "I don't want you to die before me, Mom,"
And other deep road-trip conversations.
Those are the things I will remember.
Not all the times I struggled deciding what to make for dinner
(yay for frozen pizzas and grilled cheese sandwiches!),
Or the damp towels on the bathroom floor.
Even so, I strongly suspect that I will miss all of the above,
When you're gone and on your own.

A Year in the Life of a Mom and Son: A True Story

Using humor to distract Mom

>Son: Can I watch TV after bath?
>
>Me: No, we don't have time. You'll go straight to bed.
>
>Son: Well, we're in Grandma's house, so I'll ask her.
>
>Me: (stoops down to his eye level) Son, what did I just say?
>
>Son: You know you have a hair in your mouth right now, don't you?
>
>Me: (laughs).

On Mom's youthful exploits

>Son: Tell me another story about you and my uncle when you were kids.
>
>Me: You mean like the time I convinced him that both of us should drink water from the creek near our house?
>
>Son: (laughs) Really?

Me: Yeah, and he got sick and I didn't, so I think we all know who has the better immune system now, don't we?

On falling down and being "cute"

Son: What does the word "embarrass" mean?

Me: Like, when I fell walking on the street in front of all these people. It was so embarrassing.

Son: When you were little?

Me: No, dude, this happened last year.

Son: You're not supposed to be cute when you're a grown-up!

Me: I would hardly call that "cute."

On picking up after Mom

Son: Mommy! That's it! You are not allowed to shower in my bathroom anymore!

Me: Why? What happened?

Son: I'm tired of picking all of your long hairs out of the tub!

On making fun of Mom

Me: Come here, I'm going to zip up your coat.

Son: (proceeds to blindfold his mother with her own scarf) Can you zip up my coat now? You can't, can you?

Me: (zips his coat blindfolded) I get no respect, I tell you.

On grocery shopping adventures

Son: (rummages around in the refrigerated chicken breasts, shoulder-deep).

Me: What are you doing?!

Son: I dropped my hand sanitizer here.

Me: (shakes head) OMG.

Later...

Son: (leans on paper goods).

Me: I told you not to sit on the products!

Son: I'm not sitting, I'm leaning against them.

Me: Stop being a lawyer's kid for once in your life!

Later still....

Son: (to grocery store employee) can I please have a sample of ravioli for my Mom?

Me: I can't be too upset with you now.

On Mom being a scatter-brain

On a school field trip at the aquarium:

Teacher: Kids, do you know where your adults are?

Son: Mommy!

Me: I'm here!

Son: Mommy, you're not where you're supposed to

be!

Me: Story of my life, kid. Story of my life.

On after-school car rides

Son: I want to go to my friend's house.

Me: We can't just show up at someone's house. I would have to talk to her Mommy, etc.

Son: Well, text her mommy.

Me: I'm driving. I can't text and drive.

Son: Well, I'll drive and you text.

Me: You can't drive! Do you know how old you have to be to drive?

Son: Then I'll text and you drive.

Me: Huh?

On adulting better than Mom

In the car, on the interstate...

Son: Mommy, look at this!

Me: I can't look right now because I'm driving on the...the...(having a senior moment)...

Son: Highway, we're on the highway.

Me: Yes, thank you.

On lawyering Mom

Driving Son to school, we pass a doughnut truck.

Son: Mommy! Mommy! Can we go to the doughnut shop for breakfast?

Me: No, dude I made you a stellar breakfast at home, don't you remember? We had eggs and toast.

Son: Pleeeeease, can we go to the doughnut shop now?

Me: No.

Son: Please, can we go?

Me: I said no.

Son: Please, please, please, can we go to——?

Me: Dude, I told you no.

Son: ——school. Can we go to school? Ha HA you said no!!!! So we can't go to school.

Me: (shakes head) Holy ——

On love

Son: Mommy, I hate you. It's opposite day. I really love you.

Son: (makes me a sandwich) I put four slices of meat and two slices of cheese, *with extra love.*

On The One Ring to Rule Them All

Son bought a replica of the One Ring from Lord of the Rings, which he wears around his neck.

At home, he declares, "I'm six years old, so I can have anything in the fridge that I want!"

Me: Hey, who's in charge here?

Son: (brandishes The One Ring) This ring!

Me: Well, you're not wrong.

On youth

Son: Mommy, let's play Wii, and I'll tell you what to do.

Me: What?! No one tells me what to do.

Son: That's not true. Grandma tells you what to do.

Me: (scoffs) No, she doesn't. How old am I? I'm an adult; no one tells me what to do.

Son: Well, Grandma told you what to do when you were a kid.

Me: Yes, but I'm not a kid anymore.

Son: That's not true, you're still young.

Me: (beams) I love you, Son.

On back pain

Me: We're going to the chiropractor before we go home, because my back hurts, because I am old.

Son: Mommy, you are very, very young. You're only 40.

On awesomeness

I pick him up at school. We're inside the school...

Me: Come on, dude, I promised to take you to get

pumpkins for the house. So go to the bathroom before we leave.

Son: Yay! We're going to get pumpkins?

Me: Yes.

Son: This is gonna be an awesome day!! (with a running start, he leaps and karate kicks open the swinging bathroom door).

Me: (shakes head) I will forever have this image of you stamped on my brain.

On girl things

We arrive at the grocery store...

Me: Dang, I have to pee!

Son: Seriously?

Me: Yes.

Son: Every girl in the world has to pee as soon as she leaves the house!

Me: That's right, deal with it!

On punctuality

Son: We're going to get to school late.

Me: No, we're not. We're on time.

Son: But I wanted to play outside with my friends before school starts.

Me: If you want to get to school earlier to play outside, what do you have to do?

Son: We have to drive faster.

On the Law

    Son: (singing) I fought the law, and the law won.

    Me: Of course the law won. Your mother's an attorney. To quote Judge Dredd, "I am the law!"

    Son: (shakes head).

On exorcisms

    Son: (chanting) The power of Frank compels you. (this is a line from the cartoon King Julien; Frank is a sky god).

    Me: You know the original line is, "The power of Christ compels you."

    Son: What does that mean?

    Me: It's from the movie The Exorcist.

    Son: What does it make you do?

    Me: ... ummm...it just makes you do good works (thinking, probably not appropriate to tell him that in the movie it is used to cast a demon out of a little girl. After all, I want to sleep tonight!).

    Then, we are walking around town, me dressed all in black (because that's how I roll 99.9% of the time), and Son chanting, "The power of Christ compels you."

This is my life. I swear I cannot make this stuff up.

Endless Questions

There is no limit to the curiosity of a young child:

All the clothes here have GAP written on them. Is this place called GAP?

So what happens when you die? Do you just close your eyes and fall down dead?

How is a baby born from a mommy's tummy?

Do you have a boyfriend? How old is he?

Who's your favorite Pokemon?

Were you born in the US? If you weren't, then you can't be president.

When am I going to get a baby brother?

What are we having for dinner?

Did you remember to buy (insert random product)?

When are we going to see my friends?

How about this? (then proceeds to negotiate)

You took a wrong turn. Where are we going?

If we go shopping today, can we get something for me?

Can I get a drink?

Can we go to McDonald's?

Do you like these shoes, Mommy? (after bringing me five pairs of shoes at a retail store)

Can I stay home from school with you today?
Can I go with you to your work today?
How can I help, Mommy?
What do you want for Christmas, Mommy?

Silent Revenge

The long, lean figure clad in black skulked around the perimeter of the house.

They don't know that I have a key, the figure thought.

She snickered. The sun already sunk low over the horizon. Nighttime came early this time of year.

Even better, she thought. *No one will see me enter the house.*

She had decided that her revenge would come quickly and without warning. She had had enough of the young man's tricks.

Indeed, thinking about what had happened the previous day made her clench her fists. She refused to put up with it anymore.

Inserting the key into the front door, she looked around the neighborhood before carefully pushing the door open.

A silent house greeted her, as she knew it would. After all, she had memorized the schedule of the family who lived here, making sure that no one would be home when she exacted her revenge.

A slow smile spread across her lips. The young man would never know what was coming. With luck, she would take him entirely by surprise.

She closed the door, locking it so as not to arouse suspicion.

Alone in the large foyer of the house, she looked around. All she heard were the creaky voices of an old house settling.

She crept upstairs, pulling the hood of her black jacket over her head as she did so.

The stairs groaned as she walked, but no one was around to hear the sounds.

She entered the young man's bedroom, and scoffed at the mess.

Of course he can never be bothered to clean up, she thought. *Typical.*

She smiled when she saw the area she was looking for.

A walk-in closet.

This is perfect, she thought as she rubbed her hands together.

She entered the closet and found the light switch, flicking it on.

The closet was filled to the brim with clothes, shoes, games, and electronics.

Bah, what a waste of space. She kicked a pair of sneakers out of her way.

She then became distracted by a row of brightly colored neckties.

Oh, this is grand.

She selected a necktie boasting a deep red color.

I'll exact my revenge with his own necktie.

Having thought about what she would do, she turned the light off and sat on the floor of the closet.

Now I just have to bide my time. He should be home shortly.

Indeed, after about ten minutes, she heard footsteps. She moved her head to one side, listening.

She heard the front door open in a rush.

The noises that drifted upstairs included the shuffling feet of an awkwardly proportioned boy, and the loud *whump!* of a heavy object being tossed on the ground.

Waiting in the dark, she clasped her hands together. Then, she wrapped both her hands around the necktie, stretching it taut in front of her face.

She was tall, but the young man was taller. She would have to reach high up to be able to place the necktie around his throat.

Her heart raced as she heard the stomp of footsteps coming upstairs.

Her palms became clammy as she stood up and placed herself next to the closet door.

She heard the door of the boy's room opening, then she heard shuffling dinosaur feet.

Clumsy oaf, she thought. *No worries. His clumsiness will make this easier.*

The steps became closer and she focused her eyes on the black patch where she knew the closet door was.

As she stood rooted to the floor, her back against the wall, the closet door opened. A shaft of weak light poured inside.

When she saw a hand come into the closet to throw a jacket inside, she chose that exact moment to execute her plan.

She stepped out and lunged forward, bringing the necktie up and around the young man's throat.

He automatically twisted his body around. She caught him on the side of the neck, and pulled.

The man shrieked and bent forward, but she held on and tried to clamber on top of his back.

They crashed together on the floor, and rolled to the side.

Her right hip hit the floor, but she didn't let go.

"What are you doing?!" the man yelled, hands at his throat.

"Revenge!" she cried, holding onto the necktie. "Say you're sorry!"

"Sorry for what?!"

"You ate the last of *my* Halloween candy, you moron!"

"So? It'll be Christmas in, like, two weeks!" We'll get more candy then!"

"That's not the point!" she spat in his ear. "The point is that it was *my* Halloween candy! *I* went trick or treating for it, not you! You said you were too old to go trick or treating!

"But —" he stammered.

"But what? You're not too old to eat my candy?!"

"Look, I'm sorry, all right? Get off of me!"

"You're a terrible brother!" she scoffed, standing up and throwing the necktie on the ground.

"I'll make it up to you!"

Her brother stood up and laughed hoarsely. "Thank goodness you're not strong enough to choke me for real."

His sister shot daggers at him with her eyes. "Oh, come on, you know I just wanted to freak you out a little bit."

"How'd you get in?" he asked.

"I took the spare key this morning."

"I was wondering where you were when I walked home. You ran ahead of me?"

"Yep."

"Sheesh," he said, rubbing his neck, "if I'd known you'd get so mad, I wouldn't have done it!"

"Yeah, well it better never happen again! Selfish beast!"

"Okay, okay, I'll buy you some more candy."

"You better! And none of that crap stuff, either. I expect full-size candy bars!"

"Fine," her brother said, catching his breath. "You scared the crap outta me, though."

"Good, now go get me my candy, you jerk."

Game Day

Tommy walked inside his house and dropped his backpack on the floor of the foyer. He leaned against the closed door and sighed, letting out all the pent-up, stale air from his lungs.

He loved the half hour he had to himself after school, before his older sister got home and started banging around and chatting on the phone with her friends. His parents wouldn't be home from work until almost dinnertime.

"Down, Shipwreck," he firmly but gently told the huge golden retriever who always insisted on jumping up on him as soon as he walked in the door, having been starved for attention all day.

Her original name had been Lola, but the dog was so clumsy and derpy that he and his sister had started calling her Shipwreck. The name had stuck, until the dog only responded to "Shipwreck," much to the embarrassment of their mother.

With Shipwreck at his heels, Tommy went to the kitchen and opened the sliding glass door to let the dog go outside. Next, he poured himself a big glass of ginger ale (since no one was here to tell him he couldn't have any soda) and fished around the pantry for a snack. He found potato chips and poured some into a bowl.

After he let the dog inside, he took his snack and drink up to his bedroom, settled himself on the floor, sitting against his bed, and booted up his handheld game console.

This was his favorite part of the day. No one told him what to do and what not to do. No one criticized his choice of food and drink, and no one asked him how he got that rip in the knee of his pants leg. He could relax and be alone, with no one breathing down his neck.

Tommy was almost ten years old, not old enough to be left home alone all day, according to his mother, but old enough to be alone at home for a little while. He relished these daily thirty minutes of peace like nothing else in his life.

His sister, Maya, was in her first year of high school. At fourteen years old, she seemed more woman than girl. Although they had played together as younger kids, as Maya became older she had become more and more interested in other things, such as her friends, the latest fashion, and school gossip. Tommy didn't understand her need for such external pursuits. He had plenty of fun at home by himself.

Although Maya's high school day ended earlier than Tommy's fourth-grade class, Maya typically stayed afterward to participate in different extracurricular activities. This year, she was interested in drama, and stayed late to rehearse for plays with her friends. Maya was always in the company of someone else, it seemed.

Tommy booted up Nightforce, the battle royale-style player-versus-player game with which he had been obsessed for the past year.

The game wasn't as mindless as his mother suggested. He needed to exercise extreme finger dexterity and be visually aware of several targets on the screen, all at the same time. The game necessitated accuracy and quick reflexes.

"Oh well, no one appreciates what I can do, anyway," Tommy

said aloud, with only Shipwreck listening.

He played for a while, connected to the home wi-fi network, and joined some friends from school in a squad game. As usual, Tommy carried his friends to a victory.

"Yes!" he cried, pumping one fist in the air. "Easy dub!"

Tommy downed the rest of his ginger ale and almost spilled it over his school uniform shirt when Shipwreck jumped up, gave a rapid succession of quick barks, and bolted down the stairs.

Tommy sighed. Maya was home.

He always heard her as she entered the house, chatting on the phone or to herself. Today, he heard her talking with someone, presumably on her cell phone, which their parents had bought her as soon as she had entered high school.

Didn't she see her friends at school today? Tommy thought. *Why does she have to talk to them all the time?*

Tommy heard her stomp upstairs. As she passed by the semi-open door of his bedroom, her speech became clearer.

"I think he likes her! That's what Lisa said, at least —"

Tommy rolled his eyes.

Maya saw her brother out of the corner of her eye.

Tommy made eye contact with her. "Hey," he said softly.

"Hey, bro," Maya answered. Then: "No, no, I was just talking to my brother — no, it's okay, he's busy, playing that game he always plays."

Tommy had to hand it to Maya, though. Their parents, grandparents, and even most of their cousins all made fun of him and called him antisocial because he enjoyed playing video games. But Maya never did. She didn't appear to understand him, but she wasn't derisive of him. And for that, she had his grudging respect.

Tommy relaxed and re-settled himself against his bed, this

time putting a pillow behind his back, and continued playing.

***

"Tommy! Dinner time!" His mother's shout jostled him out of his game trance.

He physically flinched at his mother's loud voice. He and Maya called it her "mom voice." Tommy wondered if his mother had had that same voice before having kids.

He met his sister on the way downstairs. She inclined her head at him.

The kids sat at the dinner table, and Tommy realized how hungry he was. Reaching over his plate toward the middle of the table, he stabbed three french fries with his fork, followed by a piece of roast chicken breast.

"Sorry I didn't have time to cook," Mom said. "But I know you guys like the chicken from that Peruvian place."

"It's cool, Mom." Maya shrugged.

"Your dad will be home later. End of the year's coming up, and you know that's a crazy time for him."

The children remained silent.

"Tommy, did you get your homework done?" Mom asked.

Tommy looked at her and nodded.

"How was school?" she continued.

"Good," he said softly.

"You had a test today, right?"

He nodded.

"How'd it go?"

"Good." He shrugged.

"What else happened at school today?"

"Not much," he answered.

"Anything interesting?"

"No." He shook his head.

Mom remained silent for a few seconds. "Nothing? You're not going to tell me about anything?"

Tommy sighed.

"Something interesting happened to *me*, Mom," Maya interrupted the conversation.

Mom's concentration broken, she turned to look at her daughter.

"Oh yeah?"

"I got picked for the play." Maya smiled broadly.

"You did? Which part?"

"Lady Macbeth!"

"That's wonderful! When will it be?"

"In a couple of months. We'll be practicing a lot so I'll have to stay after school some days, starting tomorrow."

"Well, you let me know which days, now that you can text me with your new cell phone. And I'm very proud of you."

Tommy was annoyed at his sister's hijacking the conversation to make it about her, but was simultaneously relieved that Mom no longer focused on him.

He smiled slightly at the thought of his sister being home later than usual. He didn't particularly mind her being home (except when she brought a gaggle of girlfriends with her), but he enjoyed his peaceful afternoon solitude.

Next day

As soon as Tommy arrived home, he dropped his backpack on the foyer floor as usual, grabbed a glass of water, and ran upstairs to his room.

He had been playing Nightforce for a few minutes when he heard the front door open. He froze, a deer in the headlights, and cocked his head to listen.

His shoulders automatically relaxed when he heard Shipwreck whining and jumping. That meant that Maya was home.

She's home early, he thought, lips pursed.

He listened as Maya stomped upstairs and past his door, without turning her head to look into his room.

She slammed her bedroom door shut. Tommy squinted and strained to listen.

The barking sobs were unmistakable.

Maya was crying.

Tommy felt as if he had been kicked in the gut. She wasn't trying to cramp his style by getting home early and depriving him of his alone time. She had run away from something.

He stopped playing, rose, and went to stand outside her bedroom door. He heard her now-softer sobs from outside her room, as if all of her energy were slowly being depleted. Unsure of what to do next, he tapped lightly.

The sobs stopped immediately. "What do you want?" she said through the door.

"Are you okay?" he asked.

"I'm fine!" came the angry response.

Tommy flinched and walked back to his room.

But he couldn't simply leave her that way.

What did she need? he thought.

Tommy went to the kitchen, retrieved a glass from the cup-board, and filled it with water. Crying always made him thirsty, so he figured she could use the hydration. Then he grabbed a couple of tissues from the tissue box in his room, and went back to Maya's door.

He knocked again, louder this time.

"Yes?" came the tentative response.

He gingerly opened the door and went inside.

Maya sat at her desk with her head down, and looked at him with one eye open and the other hidden beneath the crook of her elbow.

Tommy held the glass and tissues out to her. "Here," he said.

Maya lifted her face and reached for them. "Thank you."

Tommy shrugged. "Are you all right?" He couldn't think of anything else to say.

Maya shrugged in response, then took a gulp of water.

"I didn't get the role of Lady MacBeth like I thought."

Tommy furrowed his brows. "But you said yesterday that you did."

"My supposed *friend* Natalia tried out for the same role yesterday, *after* auditions were closed." She spat the word *friend* as if it were venomous.

Tommy just listened.

"Turns out," Maya continued, "she begged the drama director to let her try out, and she said that she had missed auditions because of schoolwork. Which is *bullshit* —"

Tommy blanched at the curse word. He and his sister got in huge trouble if they cursed at home.

"— because our other friend Susan said that Natalia was jealous of me and thought she could be a better Lady MacBeth, and I guess she was r-right —" Maya stammered as the tears began to flow again, "— because she g-got the part, and she knew how much I wanted it, how much I had practiced for it!"

"I'm so sorry," Tommy said. It was indeed a terrible thing to do. *Was this what high school was like?* he thought.

"It's not *your* fault," Maya said, wiping her eyes with the tissue he had brought her.

"I'm still sorry."

"She wasn't my *friend* at all. And when I saw her today and asked her about it, she acted like it was no problem. Mind you, she hadn't even considered auditioning until *after* she found out *I* got the part."

"Why did the drama director let her try out, even after auditions were closed?"

"Because she's a kiss-ass!"

"That's not fair."

"I know it's not fair!" Maya erupted, then paused. "Sorry for yelling, I'm not mad at *you*."

"Yeah, I know."

They remained in silence for a few moments, Tommy at a loss what else to do. Indeed, what could he offer his sister to make her feel better?

He could only think of one thing. It always made *him* feel better; he didn't know if it would work for her. Probably not. She would likely think it was stupid.

"Wanna play Nightforce with me?"

Maya looked at Tommy's face, and he mentally prepared himself for her to laugh at him.

"Is it fun?" she asked instead.

"*I* think it's fun." He shrugged. "And you get to kill people. You can pretend they're all Natalia."

Now Maya laughed, even as she cried, and Tommy felt good about giving her something to laugh about.

"Is it like those games we used to play a long time ago?" she asked.

Tommy loved the memories he had of he and Maya playing old Nintendo and computer games together. He had been too young to be any good back then, but she had helped him. That was before she had started to become interested in other things.

"It's different," he said. "Most of the games are different now. But it's fun, I promise."

"I heard you're really good."

Tommy felt his face reddening, embarrassed by her compliment. "I'm all right, I guess."

"Okay, sure. I think that would be fun."

They downloaded the game on Maya's phone. Since her phone was new, they hoped there wouldn't be too much lag.

"Okay," Tommy began, "this is your character. You're a no-skin, like, a default skin. If you want different skins, or clothes, you have to buy them in the online shop. But it's okay. You can play with the default skin."

Tommy showed her how to maneuver her character, how to shoot, and how to switch guns.

"Okay, now we'll start a game. We'll do a duos match, so you and I are on the same team, and we fight other duos teams."

"All right," Maya said.

"I'll mark where we land," Tommy explained.

They played the game for a while, with Maya following Tommy's lead.

"Is a tactical shotgun better than a pump shotgun?" she asked. "Which should I choose?"

"Use the tac. It's better than the pump, in my opinion, but it's not good for long range. You need like an AR or SMG to shoot people far away."

"AR?"

"Yeah, assault rifle. And SMG is for submachine gun."

"Got it."

They looted a house in the game, searching through crooks

and crannies of the rooms for goodies such as apples and bandages.

"Here," Tommy said, "take this sniper rifle. You can zoom in on players to shoot, like —" he leaned over to show her, "this."

"Oh, cool."

"Hold on, someone's outside."

Suddenly, another character entered the room they were looting. Tommy zeroed in on him and shot him, knocking him.

"Maya, finish him with the pickaxe!"

"Got it!" She complied.

"Awesome. Let's move. The storm's coming."

"Storm?"

"Yeah, see how the storm moves? You lose health in the storm, we have to stay ahead of it."

"Oh, got it. Makes sense. I mean, otherwise players could just camp and stay in the same place the whole time. The storm forces them to move in and confront each other."

"Yeah, it would be a long game if everyone just camped." Tommy laughed.

A snipe came out of nowhere.

"Sniper!" Tommy raised his voice. "West! To your left!"

"Maya maneuvered her character out of the way, biting her lower lip as she did so, with a level of concentration Tommy had rarely seen in her.

A shot rang out and the enemy fell down, knocked.

"Nice!" Tommy said. "You did it! Finish him and let's go!"

They played for a while longer, until there were only five people left in the game.

"Okay, now camp here for a while," Tommy told his sister. "Just stay here. It's a two v. two v. one. I'll take 'em out. Can you give me the rocket launcher?"

"Sure. Here." She dropped it and Tommy's character picked it up. "It only has one round of ammunition, though."

"That's all I need," Tommy said, full of bravado.

Shots rang out. Tommy's screen now indicated that there were only three remaining players.

"There's only one more guy!" he said, his movements picking up pace to mirror his excitement. "Hold on."

"Here, take this shield drink!" Maya told him.

"Thanks!" He drank it, then almost got sniped doing so.

Tommy built up to shield himself from further shots. "Maya, stay down there! Just hide!"

The last guy moved back and forth behind a building. Tommy waited, then fired the rocket launcher.

"I hit him for 50 damage! He's gotta be a one shot!"

Tommy's character zoomed out of the building and raced toward the opponent, moving around the entire time to avoid being shot.

"You're gonna die!" Maya said.

"I'll be okay," he answered. His character moved back and forth, firing off shotgun rounds at his opponent. Tommy built a wall between the two of them.

"You hardly have any health left!" Maya said.

Tommy ignored her, concentrating. "Ring around the rosy...," he sang, then fired, timing it so that the shot hit the opponent right as he landed on the ground.

A banner indicating "Victory" appeared across both Tommy's console screen and Maya's phone screen.

"YEEEEEEESSSSSSS!" Maya cried.

"Oh my God, I think that was the best game of my life!" Tommy put his hand to his chest, as if to slow his rapidly beating heart.

"Tommy, you're a beast!"

"It's no big deal," he said, shrugging.

"Shoot, you *are* really good!"

Tommy blushed. Then: "Not too bad, a win for your first game of Nightforce."

"Dang straight! Let's play again."

They played for the next couple of hours, and didn't even notice when their mother poked her head in Tommy's room.

"What are you guys doing in here?" Mom asked.

Tommy jumped. "Mom, I didn't know you were home. We're just playing Nightforce."

"Well, it's almost dinner time."

"Wait," Maya said. "It's that time already?" She checked the time on her phone. "Man, I gotta do my homework."

Their mother went downstairs as Maya rose and moved toward Tommy's door.

Once at the door, she turned around.

"Thanks," she said to her brother. "That was fun."

"No problem." Tommy nodded.

"So — game day — again — tomorrow? Same time?"

"Sure. As soon as you get home from school."

"Awesome." She smiled, and didn't look sad anymore. "I'm gonna go do my homework before Mom blows a gasket."

Tommy laughed, then turned his game console off.

Next day

Tommy and Maya met in Tommy's room the next afternoon to play Nightforce.

Maya got the hang of the game by practicing maneuvering her character.

"You're good at this!" Tommy told his sister.

"I'm all right. It *is* fun. You were right about that." She looked up at her brother briefly, then quickly refocused on her phone screen.

"I can see why you're in here playing so much," she said.

"I like playing, but it's more fun with friends, to be honest."

"So how come you use a default skin? You're way better than these other players who have all these cool skins. Is it to psyche out the other players, so they think you're a noob?"

"No." Tommy sighed. "You need gamebucks to buy skins. And for gamebucks, you need real money."

"How much does a skin cost?"

"It depends. Anywhere from, like, ten dollars to twenty-five."

"So? Why don't you use your allowance? You could save up."

Tommy shrugged. "Mom won't let me use it on gamebucks."

"Wait — what?"

He looked at his sister. "She says it's a waste of money, and I can only spend it on things that aren't a waste of money."

"But it's *your* money. You should spend it how you want. She lets *me* spend mine on *clothes.*"

"I know, and I told her that, but she said that clothes are something useful. Gamebucks aren't."

Maya huffed. "Oh please. Mom colors her hair so no one sees any grays. That's not useful. That's just her own vanity."

Tommy chuckled. "Yeah, really."

Maya continued. "Parents are so lame. Freakin' hypocritical. I mean, this is something *you like.* Who are *they* to criticize it? Do *they* see *us* criticizing the stupid sitcoms they watch, or the stupid insecure people they hang out with?"

Tommy smiled at the camaraderie his sister showed him. "It's true, they do like dumb stuff."

"And, I mean, didn't *they* play games like this when they were kids? Don't they remember what it's like?"

"I honestly don't think adults remember what it's like to have fun. They're too wrapped up in adult things. That's why they seem annoyed all the time," Tommy agreed.

"Yeah, really," Maya scoffed.

His tone became more serious. "It's all right, though. At least I get to play. My friend Mike's mom doesn't let him play video games at all. He only gets to play when he's at a friend's house and of course then he doesn't tell his mom that he plays."

Maya shook her head. "Poor guy." Then: "Oh, shoot! I wasn't paying attention! The storm's right behind me!"

"Just keep running. We've got bandages."

Seemingly out of nowhere, Maya's character fell down, struck by a sniper.

"Sniper, from the south," Maya said. "Shoot, Tommy, he got me."

"I'll save you!" Tommy hurried to move his character as quickly as he could.

"No, it's too risky. Just go."

"I can get to you."

"Just leave me! Seriously, don't risk it."

Tommy hurried over and revived Maya's character. A few seconds later, Maya was back in the game.

"Got you!" he said.

They both raced out of the storm, Maya barely escaping with her character's low health.

"Crouch here and med up. Use the bandages and shield drink."

Maya did as her brother instructed. Tommy built a structure around them, then built up to try and see where the last player in the game was hiding.

As soon as Tommy's character poked his head above his build, he got sniped.

"Oh my God! How could he kill me with one shot?!"

"It was a headshot," Maya said. "We're still in this!"

"I can play for you!" Tommy said, excited, as he moved next to his sister to watch her play on her phone screen.

"I got this," Maya said calmly.

"Just hide. He's coming," Tommy instructed. "And remember. The key to Nightforce is — relax."

Maya took a deep breath and released it.

Both children were dead silent as they heard the enemy's approaching footsteps.

The opponent took out a wall of the build and Maya replaced it quickly and built up. Then the enemy lasered the floor of her build, and her character fell.

Tommy gasped as Maya's concentration was fixed on her phone screen.

As she fell on top of the enemy she placed her remaining trap on the floor.

The enemy fell down, and the message "eliminated" appeared on the screen, followed by the Victory banner.

"Oh my God! You did it!" Tommy cried and hugged his sister with one arm. "I thought we were done for!"

"I know, me too! I was so nervous!"

"You were great!"

Maya slowed her breathing. "Shoot, my heart is beating so fast!"

"That's it," Tommy said, leaning back against his bedroom wall, satisfied by the win, "another dub!"

"You carried me — again," Maya grinned. "Until the very end, at least. Thanks for coming back for me."

"You got it." Tommy nodded. "We're a good team. You hang back and cover me while I hit the enemy head on. It works."

"Yeah." Maya seemed to consider something. "You know, if that ever happened, I mean in real life, I wouldn't want you to come try to save me. I would want you to run away."

"Really?"

"Yeah, it's better if one of us lives than if neither of us lives. You know what I mean?"

He nodded. "Okay."

"Tommy! Maya! Dinner!"

Both children scurried at the sound of their mother's voice.

Tommy and Maya rushed to the dinner table after washing their hands.

"Hey dad," Tommy said when he saw his father, glad that he was home from work on time for dinner.

"Hey, kiddo," Dad said with a smile. "It's finally Friday." He celebrated by throwing up his hands. "How are you guys doing?"

"We're good," Maya answered.

"How was work?" Tommy asked his dad.

"It was all right. You know the calendar year is closing so all my clients are doing their last-minute tax avoidance hacks."

"Yeah," Tommy agreed, even though he didn't completely understand what his father said. He was just glad Dad had time to talk with them.

"And that also means that Christmas is coming soon," Dad said, eyebrows raised.

"I can't wait!" Maya said.

"That's right," Mom said as she sat down. "Have you kids thought about what you'd like for Christmas? It's only a few weeks away."

"Yes! Tommy would like money for gamebucks!" Maya said,

her eyes popping open widely in enthusiasm.

Mom sighed, her shoulders drooping. "Sorry, but your brother and I have already talked about this."

Tommy pressed his lips together as he studied his plate of meatloaf and peas. He appreciated his sister trying, at least.

"I mean, why can't Tommy buy gamebucks with his own allowance?" Maya pressed.

"Oh, not you too!" Mom said, her mouth turning downward in annoyance. "Honestly, kids, Christmas is in a few weeks, and we'll have lots of nice presents for you, and all you can think about is stupid gamebucks?"

"Yeah, I bet you have presents we don't even like. Like sweaters and stupid crap."

"Hey —" Dad began, waving his fork in the air like a gavel.

"What's the big deal?" Maya continued. "It's *Christmas*! Shouldn't it be about what *Tommy* wants?"

"If what he wants is reasonable, yes," Mom said.

"You're a control freak," Maya said.

"Excuse me!" Mom raised her voice.

"Maya, please be respectful to your mother," Dad said evenly.

The silence was thick at the kitchen table. Tommy chanced a look at his sister, who pressed her mouth in a line, nostrils flaring as she glared at their mother. Mom, in turn, gazed stonefaced at Maya, daring her to say something else. Tommy couldn't help cracking a smile at his sister's defending him.

"Let's please calm down and eat," Dad said to nobody in particular.

"I *am* calm," Maya said through gritted teeth.

Tommy laughed; he couldn't help it. Everyone looked at him.

"What's so funny?" Mom asked.

"Nothing," he responded.

"You are," Maya huffed at their mother simultaneously.

Then both siblings proceeded to guffaw.

Mom looked angry, but then Dad put his hand on top of hers and said, "Let it go. When was the last time you saw the two of them laughing together?"

He looked into Mom's eyes and she relaxed, dropping her tensed-up shoulders.

"Well, I'm hungry," Mom said. "I'm gonna eat."

***

Later that night, right before bedtime, Maya brushed her teeth with the bathroom door open. Tommy approached cautiously.

When Maya saw her brother, she said, "Hey," through a mouthful of toothpaste.

"Just wanted to thank you for earlier," he said.

"You got it." She spit out toothpaste and rinsed. "It kills me that you're treated unfairly. I don't like it."

Tommy shrugged. "It could always be worse."

Maya turned and looked at him. Her eyes were sad.

"What?" he asked, curious.

"I think you don't stand up for yourself because you know you won't get what you want, so why bother, right?"

"I guess. So?"

"It just makes me sad, that you have a reasonable request that would make you happy and our beloved parents don't care," she said, her voice heavy with sarcasm. "I can't wait to be independent."

"Yeah, me too. Hey, tomorrow's Saturday. I usually get up early and play Nightforce and eat potato chips, since Mom and Dad sleep in. Wanna play?"

Maya beamed. "Absolutely. I'll get up as early as I can."

"Awesome," Tommy said.

"But it'll have to be just in the morning, though. I have to babysit the neighbor kid tomorrow night."

"No problem." Tommy nodded.

His sister smiled, and there was a deviousness on her face that Tommy didn't understand.

"Well, I'm gonna read for a while in my room," she said as she walked past him. "Good night, Tommy."

"Good night."

Tommy went in the bathroom to use the facilities, confused and speculating as to what his sister was planning.

Christmas Day

"Kids! Breakfast is ready! But we can open presents first!"

The children raced downstairs, taking the steps two at a time, at the sound of their mother's loud voice.

"Finally!" Tommy said.

"I know! I was so impatient!" Maya seconded.

They had been awake since six in the morning playing Night-force, remaining as silent as possible so as not to wake their slumbering parents.

Maya held up her hand and Tommy gave her a high five.

"Three dubs!" she said, and pumped a fist in the air.

Tommy laughed.

The children took their places on the living room floor near the Christmas tree. They held their breakfast plates teetering on their laps.

Loyal Shipwreck sat at Tommy's feet. He scratched the dog behind an ear and gave her a kiss on the top of her head.

Maya took a big bite of her cinnamon roll. "Umm, so good," she mumbled with her mouth full.

"Okay, kids, here are our presents to you," Mom announced, with Dad drinking coffee at her side.

Tommy and Maya began to open their gifts.

Tommy received a couple of sweaters and a pair of pajamas with the Nightforce logo emblazoned on the front.

"Thank you, Mom," he said.

"You are very welcome," his mother responded.

Maya got some teen-oriented perfume, pajamas, and a gift card for a bookstore.

"Thanks," she said to both parents.

Their mother nodded.

"Tommy!" Maya exclaimed. "Open mine next — please!"

She handed her brother a white envelope.

"What's this?" he asked.

He gazed at the envelope, enjoying the anticipation. Maya and he had never given each other Christmas presents before. Occasionally, their parents would buy things and write on the tags "to Tommy, from Maya" and "to Maya, from Tommy," but those gifts didn't count since they were picked out and paid for by their parents.

Tommy gingerly opened the envelope and removed a thick Christmas card.

The card depicted a picture of Santa playing a video game.

"I looked all over for that card," Maya told him.

Tommy smiled at her. "Thank you."

He opened the card and in his lap fell a big wad of greenbacks. His eyes widened as if he had never before seen so much money in one place.

In a trance, Tommy counted the money. There was a hundred

dollars there.

"You got him CASH?!" Mom exclaimed.

"Yeah, so?" Maya shrugged. "I saved it from my babysitting jobs."

"It's so *impersonal*," Mom said. "Not really appropriate for Christmas."

Maya looked her mother in the eye. "Who are *you* to say what's appropriate for Christmas? It's what he wanted, if you would have actually listed to him for once."

"Oh my God!" Tommy cried. "Thank you!" He looked at his sister. "Thank you so much!"

He got up, ran to Maya, and threw his arms around her. She hugged him back. His heart beat a mile a minute in his chest.

"I'm glad you like it," Maya said, leaning back with a wide grin on her face. She then turned and gave their parents a hard stare.

"He gets to spend it on whatever he wants, *even gamebucks*."

"I don't know —" Mom began.

Dad finally chimed in. "Come on, Sharon, it's Christmas."

Their mother sighed, her shoulders falling at once. "All right, just this once."

Tommy stood up. "Come on, Maya. I want to buy some skins now." Then he frowned. "But I can't use cash. I need a credit card."

"We can use mine. The one Mom gave me for emergencies." She stood and looked at her mother. "This is an emergency. It's *Christmas*."

Her mother pursed her lips together, but said nothing.

Tommy shifted from foot to foot, as if he had a ton of pent-up energy.

"I don't even know what skins I'm going to get! Maya, want

to help me pick them out?"

Maya smiled from ear to ear. "You got it."

The children raced out of the living room and up the stairs, leaving the remainder of their presents unwrapped under the Christmas tree. Shipwreck barked at the rush of movement and followed them, running up the stairs at their heels.

"What about the rest of your presents?!" Mom called after them.

"We'll get to them later!" Maya yelled back. "It's game day!"

"Yeah, Mom!" Tommy called. "Right now we just wanna play Nightforce!"

THE END

Thank you so much for reading. I would very much appreciate if you posted an honest review on Amazon and/or Goodreads.

If you would like to hear about my forthcoming short stories and fiction and nonfiction books, you can sign up for my update list here.

About the Author

Maria Riegger is based in the Washington, DC area. She is a banking/corporate attorney by day (but please don't hold that against her), and an author by night.

Maria is a Gemini whose head has always been in the clouds. From a young age, her mother scolded her for not paying attention; when she was bored, she would make up stories in her head. She has been writing since she was about thirteen years old. A lover of languages, she speaks French, Spanish, and Catalan.

She has been caught air-guitaring in public. She loves to laugh, and is the "go-to" person if a friend needs someone to laugh at his lame jokes. In true Gemini fashion, she indulges both her logical personality as an attorney as well as her creative fiction-writing personality. She loved law school and even misses it, which led her friends to conclude that she is certifiable.

An irreverent Gen X'er, she writes gritty contemporary romance, with plenty of sarcasm, as well as nonfiction.

You can connect with me on:

- http://www.lawschoolheretic.com
- http://www.twitter.com/RieggerM
- http://www.facebook.com/lawschoolheretic
- http://www.instagram.com/rieggemr

Subscribe to my newsletter:

- http://eepurl.com/dAz9HH

Also by Maria R. Riegger

I write irreverent fiction and nonfiction.

Miscalculated Risks

http://www.lawschoolheretic.com/shop

She's an overachieving law student who's not looking for love, so why can't she resist the mysterious new-comer?

Outspoken and abrasive, law student Isabel enjoys arguing with just about everyone, including her friends. Her strained relationship with her mother, less-than-stellar job prospects and frustrations with the conformist culture of Washington, DC have left her resentful and unfulfilled. When she meets Tarek, a new fellow student who dares to challenge her, she is intrigued but skeptical. While Isabel is risk-averse where her feelings are concerned, she is also becoming increasingly curious. She's afraid to get close, because being vulnerable always lead to being hurt, doesn't it?

Acceptable Misconduct

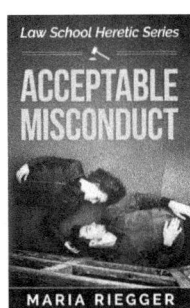

http://www.lawschoolheretic.com/shop

In the sequel to Miscalculated Risks, antagonistic Washington DC law student Isabel must face her unsettled past and navigate the final weeks of the semester while figuring out fellow student Tarek's feelings for her before he slips away. Will Isabel be willing and able to reveal her painful secret, at the risk of losing the one man who truly understands her?

Thunderstruck

http://www.lawschoolheretic.com/shop

They're opposing candidates in a contentious election who have a scandalous past.

Years ago, Monica and Brian had an intense affair, which ended in heartbreak.

Years later, Monica ends up facing Brian in a congressional campaign on the outskirts of Washington, DC. Old sentiments resurface, threatening to derail Monica's political plans. And when everything becomes public, Monica turns into a woman with nothing to lose. She's determined to win the election at any cost, despite whatever she may be feeling for her opponent. As Brian deals with his feelings for the only woman who ever really understood him, he is forced to make a decision about revealing information that could help him, but destroy her. As oversized egos and the desire to win an election threaten the bond slowly forming between these two political opponents, they end up discovering that they may have more in common than they originally thought.

Your Scorpio Child

Want to know all the secrets to handling your intense Scorpio child?

Scorpio is the most misunderstood and enigmatic of all the signs in the zodiac. Much has been written about Scorpio men and women. However, the Scorpio child remains elusive, mostly because Scorpio children do not usually say what is on their mind. Scorpio children are dramatic, suspicious, manipulative, and can seriously try parents' patience. The key to having the relationship with your Scorpio child that you want lies in knowing how to handle his innate characteristics. I hope that you find the information in this book useful.

Self-Publishing Primer

https://lawschoolheretic.com/free-stuff

I'm giving away a self-publishing guide FOR FREE.

I'm a self-published author who's been in the trenches. Let me help you. You'll get all the relevant info in one spot! I learned how to self-publish on the fly, and I'd like to let you in on what I know. This information is so essential that I want you to have it for FREE.